A Creepy Countdown

BY **CHARLOTTE HUCK**

PICTURES BY **JOS. A. SMITH**

Greenwillow Books
New York

One tall scarecrow standing on a hill.

TWO lumpy toads sitting very still.

Four hooting owls,
their eyes burning bright.

Five furry bats hanging

upside down.

Six skinny witches
flying through the town.

Seven ghastly ghosts rising from their bed.

Nine eerie skeletons dancing on a grave.

Ten tiny mice,
feeling very brave,

squeaked

BOO

Ten laughing mice scampered to their nest.

Nine eerie skeletons laid their bones to rest.

Eight yowling cats arched their backs and fled.

Seven
ghastly ghosts
sank into their bed.

Six
skinny witches
flew to their lair.

Five black bats swept through the air.

Four silent owls glided off in flight.

Three
jack-o'-lanterns
dimmed their glowing light.

One tall scarecrow
stood all alone.

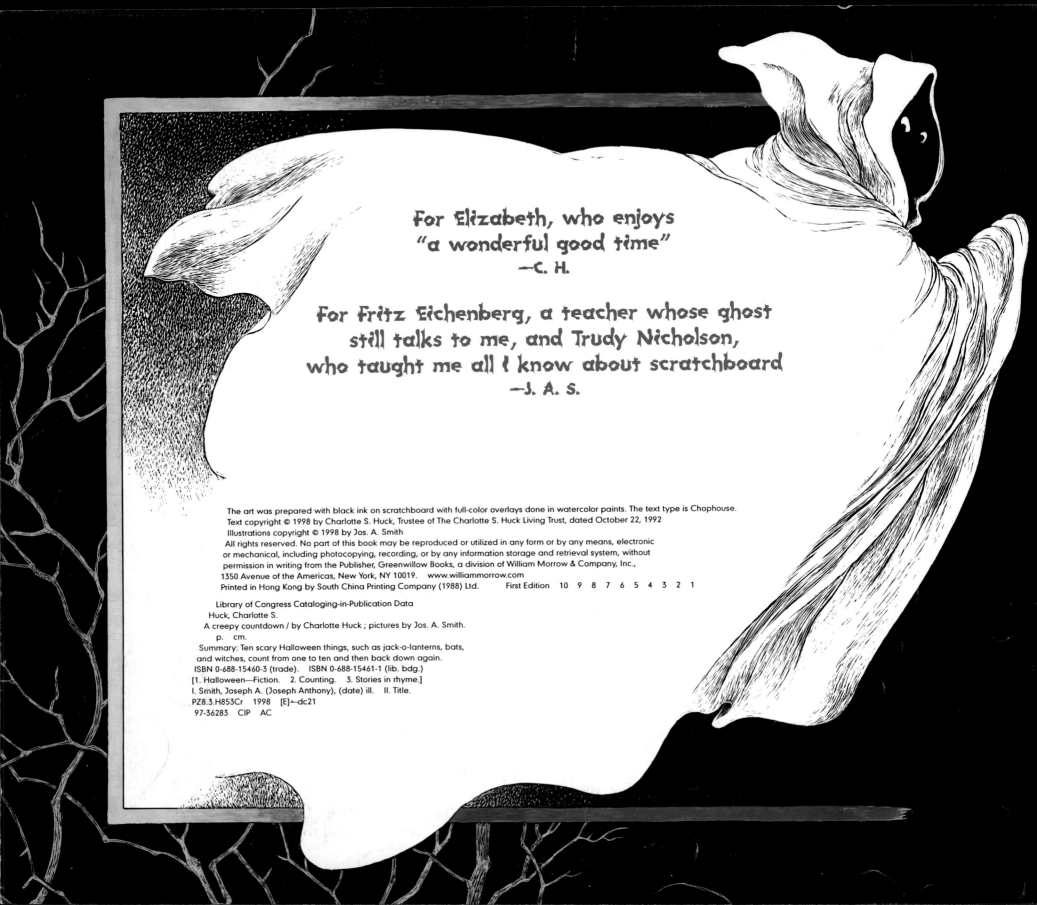

For Elizabeth, who enjoys
"a wonderful good time"
—C. H.

For Fritz Eichenberg, a teacher whose ghost
still talks to me, and Trudy Nicholson,
who taught me all I know about scratchboard
—J. A. S.

The art was prepared with black ink on scratchboard with full-color overlays done in watercolor paints. The text type is Chophouse.
Text copyright © 1998 by Charlotte S. Huck, Trustee of The Charlotte S. Huck Living Trust, dated October 22, 1992
Illustrations copyright © 1998 by Jos. A. Smith
Printed in Hong Kong by South China Printing Company (1988) Ltd.   First Edition   10 9 8 7 6 5 4 3 2 1

Library of Congress Cataloging-in-Publication Data
Huck, Charlotte S.
A creepy countdown / by Charlotte Huck ; pictures by Jos. A. Smith.
     p.   cm.
Summary: Ten scary Halloween things, such as jack-o-lanterns, bats,
and witches, count from one to ten and then back down again.
ISBN 0-688-15460-3 (trade).   ISBN 0-688-15461-1 (lib. bdg.)
[1. Halloween—Fiction.   2. Counting.   3. Stories in rhyme.]
I. Smith, Joseph A. (Joseph Anthony), (date) ill.   II. Title.
PZ8.3.H853Cr   1998   [E]—dc21
97-36283   CIP   AC